The Three Billy Goats Gruff

©2004 Alligator Books Limited
Gadd House, Arcadia Avenue
London N3 2JU

Printed in China

Once upon a time there were three billy goats. First there was the little billy goat Gruff, who was the smallest of the three.

Then there was the middle billy goat Gruff, who was bigger than the little billy goat Gruff, but not as big as the great big billy goat Gruff.

And he was, as you can see, the biggest of them all!

Now these billy goats lived in a tiny village at the foot of a high mountain.

Every year during spring and summer, the three billy goats Gruff left their tiny village and went to stay up on the hillside nearby.

All day they nibbled the juicy green grass that grew there, and by night they slept underneath the stars.

Some days the three billy goats Gruff crossed the river to the other side of the valley, where the grass was even greener and juicier and full of sweet-smelling wild flowers.

Now the bridge over the river was rickety-rackety. It swayed and creaked and went wibbly-wobbly.

"Perhaps someone will mend it one fine day," said the three billy goats Gruff every time they went trip-trapping across.

But when winter came along and snow covered the juicy green grass, the three billy goats Gruff said goodbye to the hillside, and went back to live in their tiny village at the foot of the high mountain.

So every year before the weather got too cold and the snow was too deep, the three billy goats Gruff trotted home down the mountain track.

The folks in the village were delighted to see them, especially the children. For it was their job to look after the three billy goats Gruff in winter.

Sometimes the children gave them oats to nibble from a basket, and barley from a big brass bucket.

The little billy goat Gruff, as you can see, would nibble anything that came his way!

But the three billy goats Gruff were happiest of all when the children brought them sweet-smelling hay. It reminded them of the juicy green grass that grew on the hillside in springtime.

And through the long dark winter nights, when the three billy goats Gruff were nice and warm and cosy in the barn, the children would listen to stories.

When the shutters were closed tight and the fire was burning brightly, that was the time the children wanted to hear about...TROLLS!

Now there are trolls with claws and rows of teeth!
There are trolls with horns and great big feet!
Some of them are scaly! Some of them are hairy!
But every troll is...BIG, BAD AND SCARY!

The children listened to tales of trolls until it was past their bedtime.

"Goodnight and beware of the big bad trolls," they whispered sleepily as they went off to bed.

They hide under bridges,
In dark caves and holes.
Don't go up the mountain,
For fear of the TROLLS!

Now the three billy goats Gruff never heard all the stories that were told about the trolls on dark winter nights.

Which was just as well perhaps!

On winter nights, as soon as darkness fell, all the animals in the warm cosy barn settled down to sleep.

The three billy goats Gruff closed their eyes and dreamed of spring, when the juicy green grass would grow on the hillside once more.

Then one very special morning, as the three billy goats Gruff came out of the barn...something felt different!

Birds were whistling, bees were humming and a sunbeam tickled the little billy goat Gruff's nose... SPRING HAD COME AT LAST!

"I can smell spring!" and the middle billy goat Gruff sighed as he sniffed the fresh air.

"It must be the new juicy green grass on the hillside you can smell!" said the great big billy goat Gruff.

So, without wasting a single moment, the three of them trotted out of the tiny village, and turned up the narrow path that led to the hillside.

When the three billy goats Gruff saw the new grass, it made them feel hungry, and they began to nibble the fresh shoots straight away.

They chomped and they munched, they chewed and they crunched all morning long, until every single bit of the juicy green grass had vanished.

"Where's it all gone?" gasped the little billy goat Gruff as he stared at the ground.

"We've eaten it, I'm afraid!" said the middle billy goat Gruff sadly.

"Look across the river!" cried the great big billy goat Gruff. "There's a whole hillside covered with new juicy green grass over there!"

The three billy goats Gruff could hardly wait to cross over the bridge and get to the new juicy green grass on the other side.

"I wonder if the bridge is still rickety-rackety?" asked the little billy goat Gruff as they rushed down to the river.

"I wonder if the bridge still sways and creaks and goes wibbly-wobbly?" asked the middle billy goat Gruff.

"I wonder if our hooves still go trip-trap every time we cross the bridge?" asked the great big billy goat Gruff.

"I'm the smallest! I'll go first!" called the little billy goat Gruff. "Then we'll find out!"

And off he went.

Now the three billy goats Gruff didn't know that during the long cold dark months of winter, a BIG BAD TROLL had come to live beneath the rickety-rackety bridge.

The instant he heard the little billy goat Gruff's small hooves trip-trapping across the wibbly-wobbly wooden planks, the big bad troll leapt out from under the rickety-rackety bridge.

He raged! He roared! He showed his claws!

He gnashed his pointed teeth!

"I'll eat anyone I catch trip-trapping across my bridge!" he growled fiercely.

The little billy goat Gruff stood quite still. He didn't shake! He didn't quake! He didn't scream or shiver!

Instead he looked at the big bad troll and said, "My brother is much bigger than me. He'll make a better supper!"

So the big bad troll let the little billy goat Gruff go. And he went trip-trapping across the rickety-rackety bridge to the other side.

And there he stayed munching the juicy green grass as he waited for his brothers.

Next to cross the rickety-rackety bridge was the middle billy goat Gruff, who was bigger than the little billy goat Gruff, but not as big as the great big billy goat Gruff.

The instant the big bad troll heard the middle billy goat's hooves trip-trapping across the wibbly-wobbly wooden planks, he leapt out from under the rickety-rackety bridge.

He raged! He roared! He showed his claws! He gnashed his pointed teeth!

"I'll eat anyone I catch trip-trapping across my bridge!" he growled fiercely.

The middle billy goat Gruff stood quite still. He didn't shake! He didn't quake! He didn't scream or shiver!

Instead he looked at the big bad troll and said, "My brother is much bigger than me. He'll make a better supper!"

So the big bad troll let the middle billy goat Gruff go.
And he went trip-trapping across the rickety-rackety bridge to the other side.

And there he stayed munching the juicy green grass as he waited for his great big brother.

Now the big bad troll had made such a din, and hollered so loudly, that the great big billy goat Gruff realised what was happening.

And he knew just what to do!

The instant the big bad troll heard the great big billy goat Gruff's hooves on the wibbly-wobbly wooden planks, he leapt up onto the rickety-rackety bridge.

Then he opened his mouth wide and yelled, "You're big enough for my supper!"

"Oh no, I'm not!" snorted the great big billy goat Gruff.

Then he put down his huge sharp horns and he charged CRASH! BANG! WHAM!

The big bad troll whizzed high into the air, then flew over the mountains roaring and hollering.

Where he landed, I can not tell, but he never came back again!

When the folks in the tiny village learned that the big bad troll had gone for ever, they wanted to thank the billy goats Gruff for being so brave and clever.

So they decided to celebrate.

It was the children's idea to have a grand picnic in honour of the three billy goats Gruff.

And everybody agreed.

So the very next afternoon, (when the rickety-rackety bridge had been mended at last!) everyone trooped over the river to the hillside.

The three billy goats Gruff ate plenty of oats from a basket, and lots of barley from a brass bucket.

And the little billy goat Gruff nibbled anything that came his way!

And the big bad troll, wherever he landed, must have told all the other trolls...never, never, under any circumstances whatsoever, go near the three billy goats Gruff!